A Gift for You from
Seward Child Care Center
2323 32nd Ave. S.
Minneapolis, MN 55406

CLICK, CLACK, Splish, Splash

A Counting Adventure

by doreen cronin
and
betsy lewin

atheneum books for young readers

NEW YORK LONDON TORONTO SYDNEY

1 farmer sleeping.

2 feet creeping.

3 buckets piled high.

4
chickens
standing
by.

5 cows type a note.

6 goats load the boat.

7 pigs lead the way.

8 sheep decide to stay.

9

mice
leave
a
note
on
the
door.

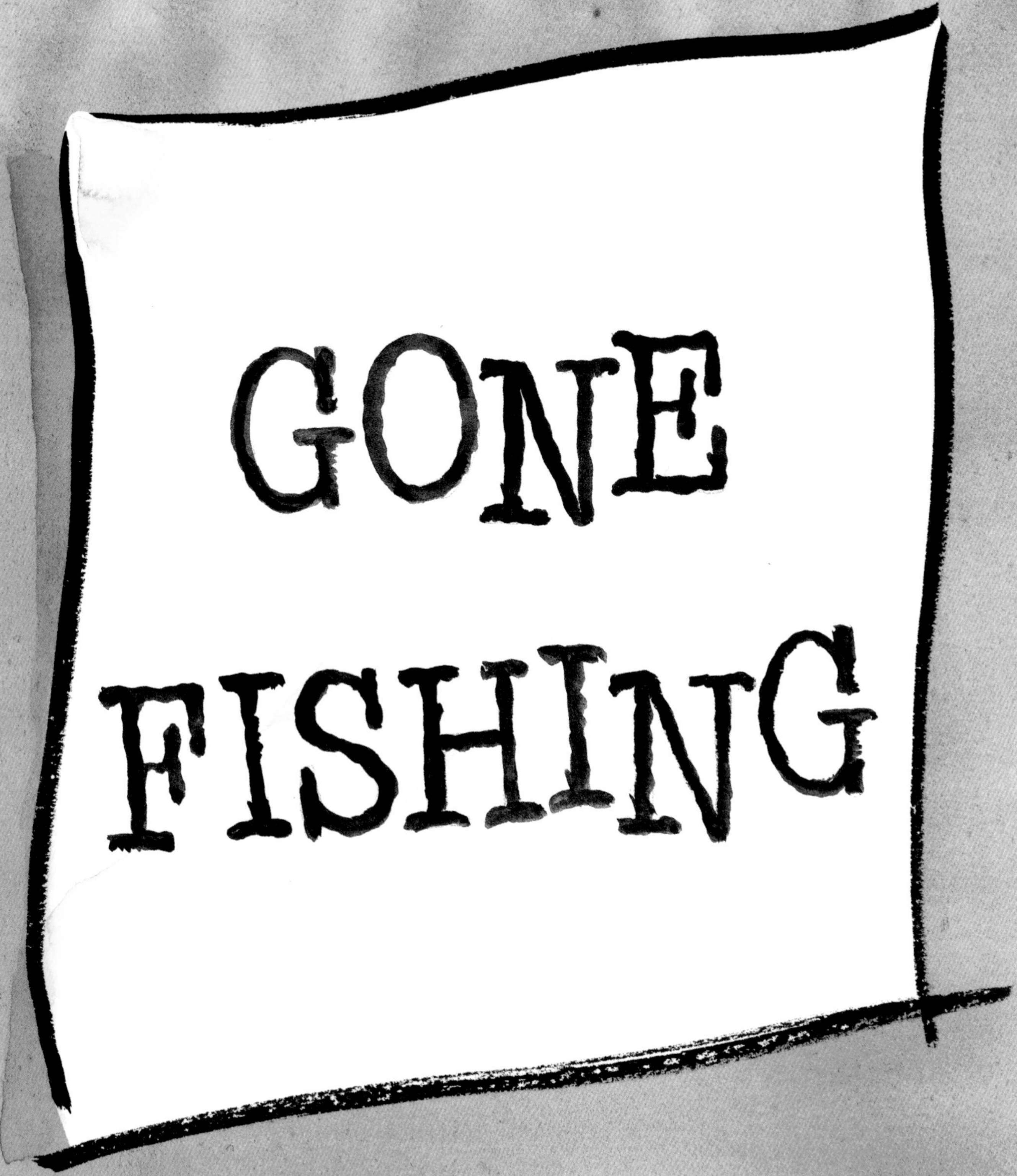
GONE
FISHING

All the animals

go to the shore.

10 buckets lined up in a row.

10 fish ready to go.

One sleepy farmer rubs his eyes
and wakes up to a fishy surprise!

For Julia
—D. C.

To Julia again, and to Grace Isabelle—
have a great childhood!
—B. L.

Atheneum Books for Young Readers
An imprint of Simon & Schuster Children's Publishing Division
1230 Avenue of the Americas
New York, New York 10020
Text copyright © 2006 by Doreen Cronin
Illustrations copyright © 2006 by Betsy Lewin
Book design by Ann Bobco
The text for this book is set in Filosofia.
The illustrations for this book are rendered in brush and watercolor.
Manufactured in the United States of America
First Edition
10 9 8 7 6 5 4 3 2 1
Library of Congress Cataloging-in-Publication Data
Cronin, Doreen.
Click, clack, splish, splash: a counting adventure / Doreen Cronin ; illustrated by Betsy
Lewin.—1st ed.
p.   cm.
Summary: While Farmer Brown sleeps, some of the animals who live on
the farm go on a fishing expedition.
ISBN-13: 978-0-689-87716-2
ISBN-10: 0-689-87716-1
[1. Animals—Fiction. 2. Farmers—Fiction. 3. Fishing—Fiction.
4. Counting. 5. Stories in rhyme.]
I. Title: Click, clack, one two three. II. Lewin, Betsy, ill. III. Title.
PZ8.3.C879Cl 2006
[E]—dc22   2004029020